Superman™

Robo Monster

Copyright © DC Comics 2008. First Edition,
Printed in The United States of America. All rights reserved.
ISBN: 978-0-696-23957-1

We welcome your comments and suggestions.
Write to us at: Meredith Books, Children's Books,
1716 Locust Street, Des Moines, IA 50309-3023

Visit us at: meredithbooks.com

Written by Jake Black
Illustrated by Scott Stewart

The sun was shining brightly, and the people of Metropolis were enjoying the day. Lex Luthor had announced that he was going to unveil the newest addition to the city's Natural History Museum— a gigantic robotic dinosaur.

Lois Lane and Clark Kent stood in the crowd, paying close attention to Lex and his dinosaur. They were reporting on the big news for the *Daily Planet*.

Clark had a secret. He was not only a great reporter, he also was Superman. People all over the world loved Superman because he always fought for truth and justice.

"What do you think Lex is going to say about the dinosaur?" Lois asked.

Clark glared at Lex. "I don't know, Lois. I don't trust him," he replied.

Lex Luthor stood behind a podium, looking over the large crowd. Many people in Metropolis liked Lex. They didn't know that he was the most dangerous criminal mind in the world. But Superman knew.

"My friends! Welcome to the Metropolis Natural History Museum!" Lex said. "We're here today to show off LexCorp's latest contribution to the world of science and technology. This new robot will show visitors at the museum how dinosaurs moved and lived."

Lex pressed a button on the podium, and a huge curtain opened behind him. There stood the gigantic tyrannosaurus rex robot. The audience all gasped, amazed at the massive creature.

"Wow, Clark. That's pretty impressive," Lois said.

"And now another small demonstration," Lex said as he pushed a different button. The gigantic dinosaur moved its head and arms, letting out a mighty roar. "You see, with its realistic movement and sound, this robot will be a great educational tool," Lex said.

Suddenly, the dinosaur started moving toward the audience. Its large feet came crashing down on the sidewalk, shaking the ground. Everyone was scared.

"Something's wrong! It shouldn't be doing this!" Lex yelled.

The crowd scattered to get out of the dinosaur's way. Lois started to run too. "Clark! Where are you?" she screamed. "We need to get out of here!" But Clark was nowhere to be seen.

The dinosaur stomped down the street. Its giant tail smashed buildings as it passed.

"Look! Up in the sky!" someone yelled. A blue-and-red blur was flying toward the robot monster.

Superman flew through the air, heading for the dinosaur. He could see the mob of people on the street below and knew he had to stop Lex's robot before anyone got hurt.

Lois stopped running and looked up at
Superman. She was always happy when
Superman showed up to save the day.
Distracted, she didn't notice that the
dinosaur's huge foot was coming down
on top of her until it was too late.

With a burst of speed, Superman swooped in and carried Lois to the safety of a nearby rooftop.

"Thanks, Superman!" Lois said.

"You're safe here, Lois. I've got a dinosaur to stop!" Superman called as he soared toward the giant robot.

Superman focused his X-ray vision on the dinosaur to look inside its metal shell at the robot's wiring.

Its advanced technology is going make it much harder to stop, Superman thought.

Superman hovered in front of the dinosaur's face. Glaring at the monster he said, "This ends here!"

The dinosaur roared and swung its massive tail at Superman.

The tail hit Superman with astounding force, but using his superstrength, the Man of Steel stopped the blow. He held the tail tightly in his arms, snapping it off. Electrical sparks and flames flew from the metallic wound.

With a gust of superbreath,
Superman put out the fire.
But the dinosaur continued
destroying the city!

Superman focused his eyes on the dinosaur's main computer. Two streams of heat vision shot from Superman's eyes, cutting through the monster's metal skin.

Finally, the gigantic robot stopped walking. But now it was falling over!

As the dinosaur crashed toward the ground, Superman sped beneath it. He caught the falling beast in the nick of time.

The people cheered, but Superman's superhearing picked up someone yelling in the distance, "No! The dinosaur was supposed to *beat* Superman!" It was Lex Luthor.

Superman raced back to the museum and grabbed Lex. "Your dinosaur caused a lot of problems today, Luthor," Superman said as he carried his enemy through the air. "I heard your plan, and you're going to jail."

A short while later, Clark Kent walked into the *Daily Planet* newsroom. Lois was telling everyone about Superman destroying the dinosaur. Clark listened intently to Lois' story and smiled. As Superman, he'd saved the day again. It was a good feeling!

ATTENTION, METROPOLIS CITIZENS!

Lex Luthor has hidden the items below throughout Metropolis. We here at the *Daily Planet* are asking you to help Superman find them. Be careful—these items are dangerous, and one of them is hidden on each page.

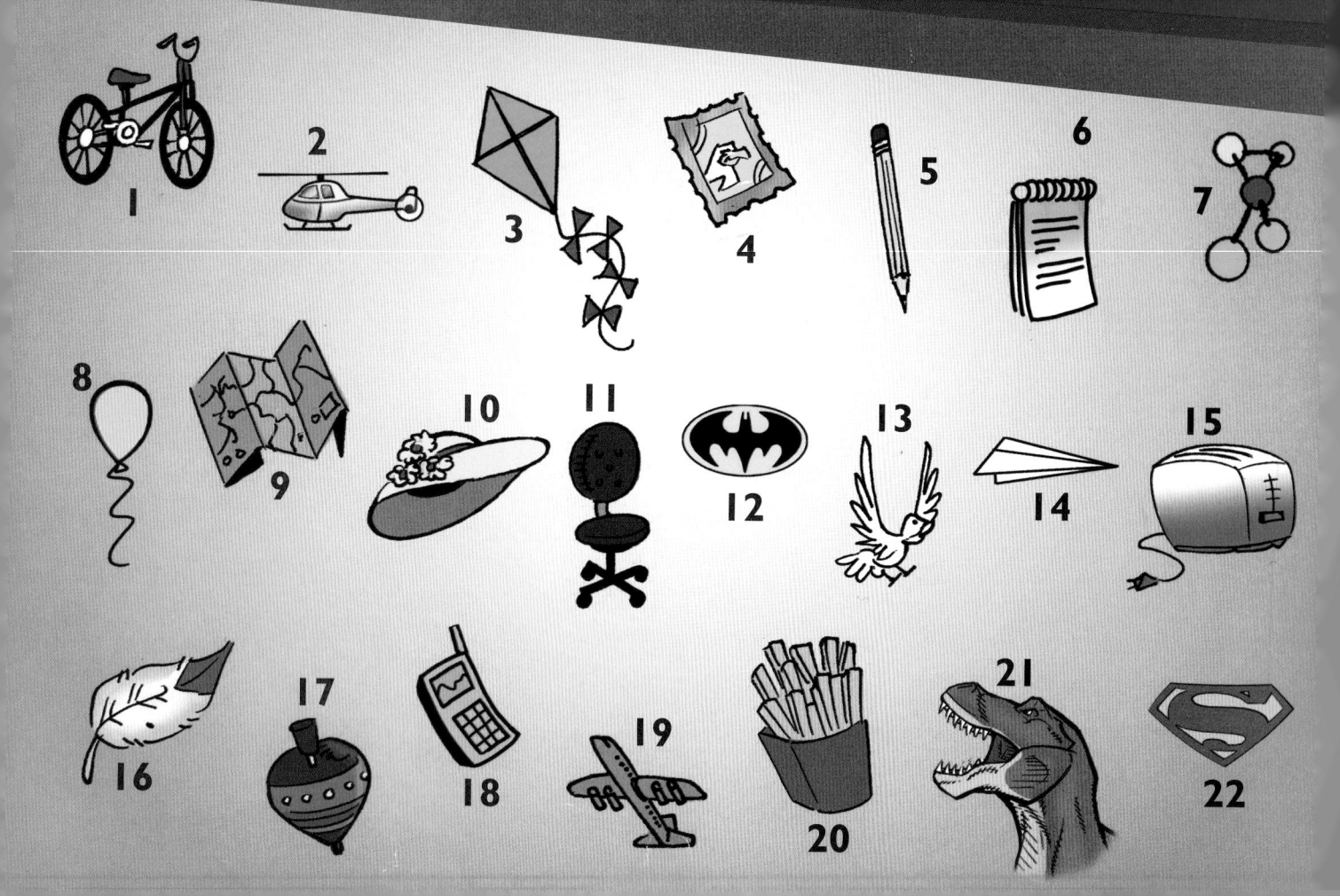

1
2
3
4
5
6
7
8
9
10
11
12
13
14
15
16
17
18
19
20
21
22